Dogs Don't Wear Glasses

by

ADRIENNE GEOGHEGAN

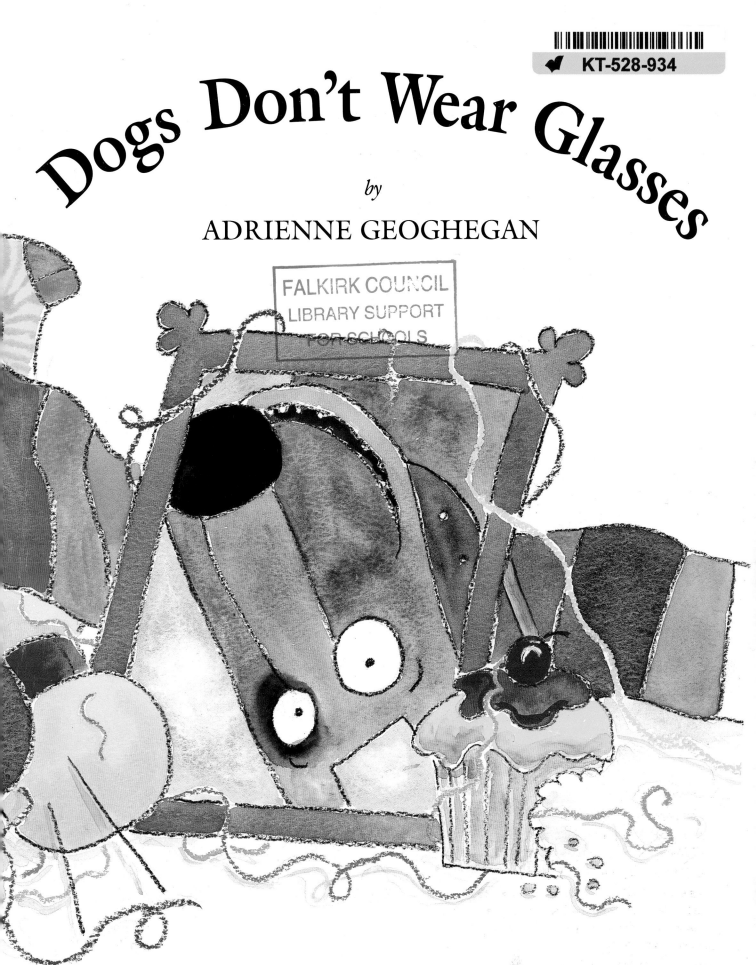

MAGI PUBLICATIONS

London

Nanny Needles spent most of her time in bed, knitting sweaters.

D
OGS
DON'T
WEAR
GLASSES

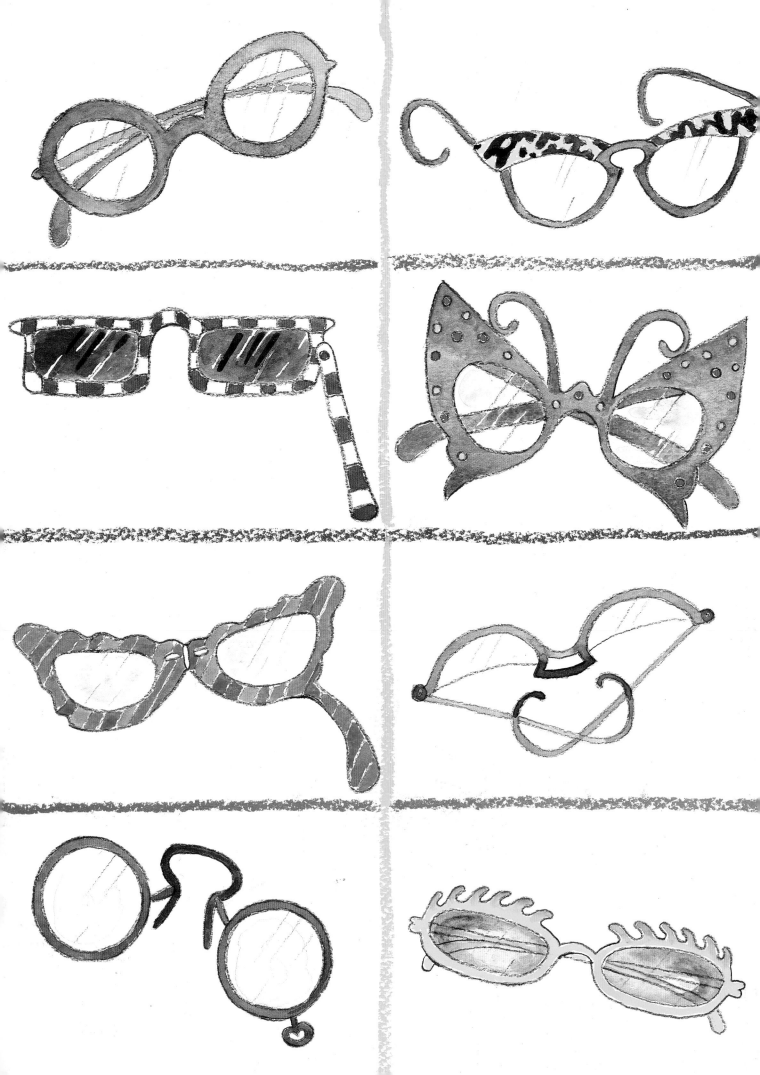

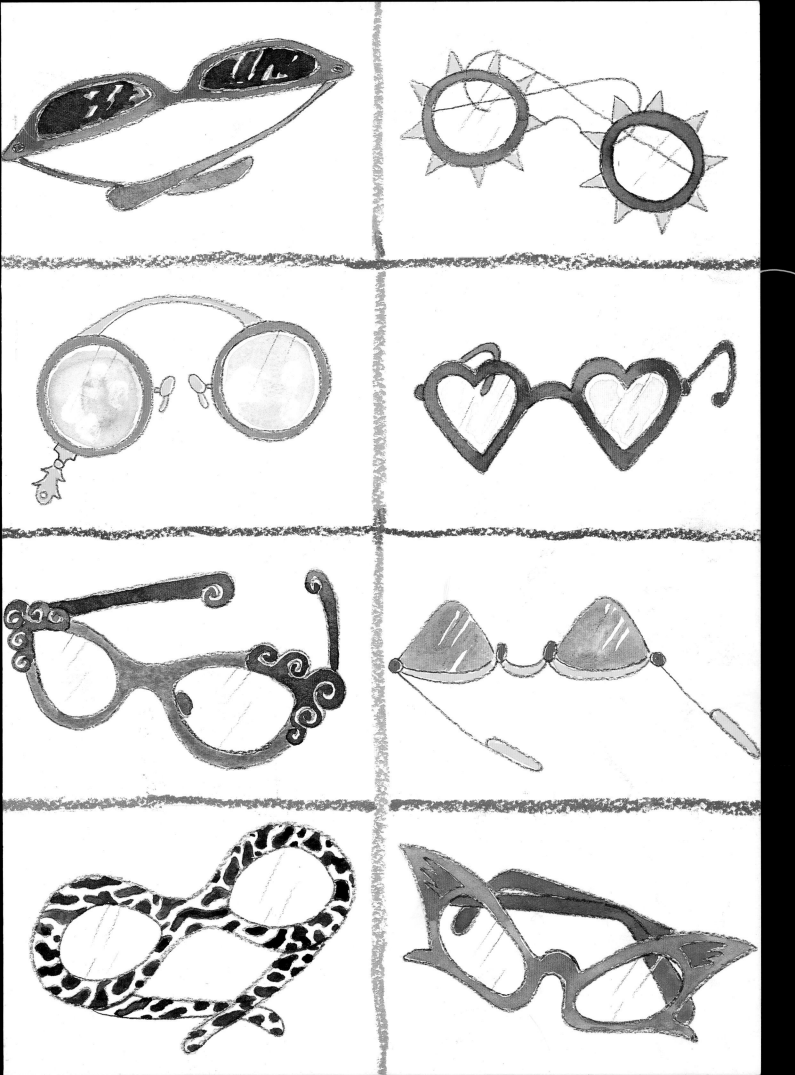

For Mum and Dad

– miss you

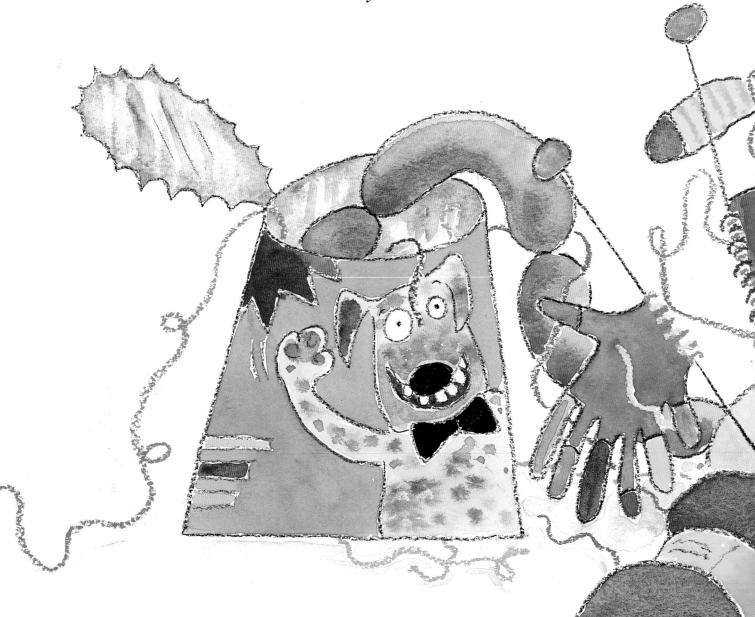

Reprinted 1998

This paperback edition published 1997

First published in 1996 by Magi Publications
22 Manchester Street, London W1M 5PG

© 1996 by Adrienne Geoghegan

Adrienne Geoghegan has asserted her right
to be identified as the author and illustrator of
this work under the Copyright, Designs and
Patents Act, 1988.

Printed in Italy by Grafiche AZ, Verona

ISBN 1 85430 411 9

Seymour, her dog, was perfectly happy with this arrangement.

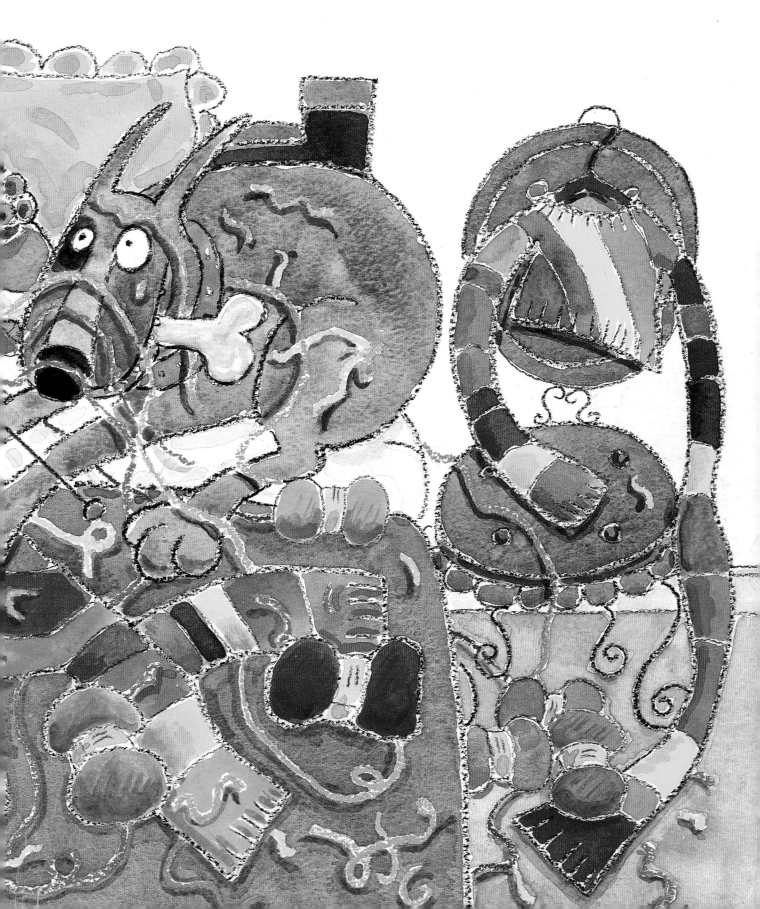

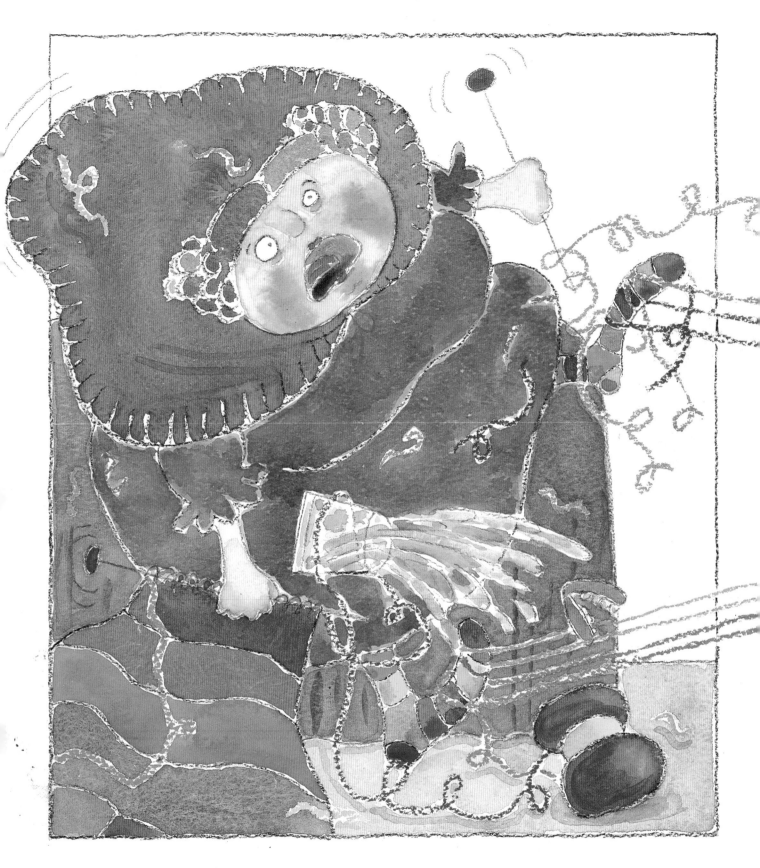

One day Nanny Needles was feeling rather sprightly,
so she hopped out of bed. As she did so, her wool got
tangled up with Seymour's bone.

"You dim dog!" she shouted. "Don't bring that stinking
filthy bone into bed again!"
Seymour growled a little growl, and ran off into the
kitchen to keep out of Nanny's way . . .

. . . but Nanny Needles got there first.
She began to sweep the floor. She scrubbed and
she swept and she shined. She went to tip
the rubbish into the bin . . .

. . . SPLASH! SPLODGE!
SPLUTTER!

She missed!
The whole mess landed on Seymour's head.
He licked the good bits off.
"You clumsy dog!" she scolded. "You must watch
where you sit. Perhaps you need your eyes tested."

Seymour crept up to his bed, next to Nanny Needles'
washing basket, and hid his bone under the blankets.

"I think I'll do my washing now, while that dog is out from under my feet," thought Nanny Needles.

To Seymour's horror, Nanny Needles bunged all *his* things into the washing machine – his bone, his blanket, his pillow and his chewed slipper.

They all spun round and round in the warm sudsy water.
After the machine stopped, Nanny Needles opened it to
remove her washing . . .

. . . but all she found was a tinchie winchie bone, a handkerchief blanket, a pincushion pillow and one chewed-up little slipper.

"This is *your* stuff, Seymour," she shouted. "But where's *my* washing?"

Nanny Needles felt exhausted.

"Oh, Seymour, whatever will I do with you?" she cried. "Perhaps your hair is getting in your eyes? I know! I'll give you a haircut."

But she cut too much off the top of Seymour's head,
and left him with a large pink bald spot.

Seymour ran off, and hid under the bed
for a nice quiet nap. He woke up to the sound
of the tin opener.
"Mm, dinner," he thought. But to his amazement,
Nanny Needles gave him . . .

. . . sausages, beans and chips on a china plate.
She sat down, and tucked into a bowl of Beef and Liver
for Healthy Dogs.

Afterwards, she felt a bit queasy.
When she had recovered, she looked at her empty bowl.
"Oh, no! What have I eaten?" she cried. *"And where are
my sausages?"*

Seymour was hiding under Nanny Needles' bed again.

"Have you eaten my sausages?" cried Nanny Needles.
"I'm not blaming you, though. It's your eyes. I think you
need them tested, so that you can see more, Seymour."

So next day off they went to the opticians.

"Sorry," said Mr Lensman. "Dogs don't wear glasses."
"But he can't see a thing," said Nanny Needles. "He bumps into everything and he eats my sausages and mixes up my washing and . . . and . . ."
"*All right, all right,*" said Mr Lensman. "He can have an eye test."

The eye test went perfectly, but Nanny Needles still insisted that Seymour needed glasses.

"Try these," said Mr Lensman.
Seymour felt seasick.

"What about these nice modern
mauve ones," said Nanny Needles.
But when Seymour looked through
them, everyone seemed so skinny,
they almost disappeared.

"Ooh, I like those green tinted ones,"
said Nanny Needles. Seymour looked
into the mirror, but appeared a little
bit froggy!

"These blue ones are on special offer," said Mr Lensman.
Seymour didn't like them. They clashed with his pink scalp.
Nanny Needles felt differently.
"Oh, Seymour," she cried. "What lovely blue frames. They
really do suit your colouring." Before Seymour could protest,
Nanny Needles had bought them.

"Now put them on," said Nanny Needles, when they
arrived home.
But Seymour refused to wear them.
"Would you like me to try them first?" she coaxed.
"Then you can see how smart they look."
So Nanny Needles tried them on, and looked in the mirror . . .

"Goodness!" cried Nanny Needles. "Everything looks so
big and bright and wonderful!"
Then she looked at Seymour.

"Why, Seymour," she said. "You've grown quite bald and fat in your old age. Perhaps you need to go on a *diet*!"

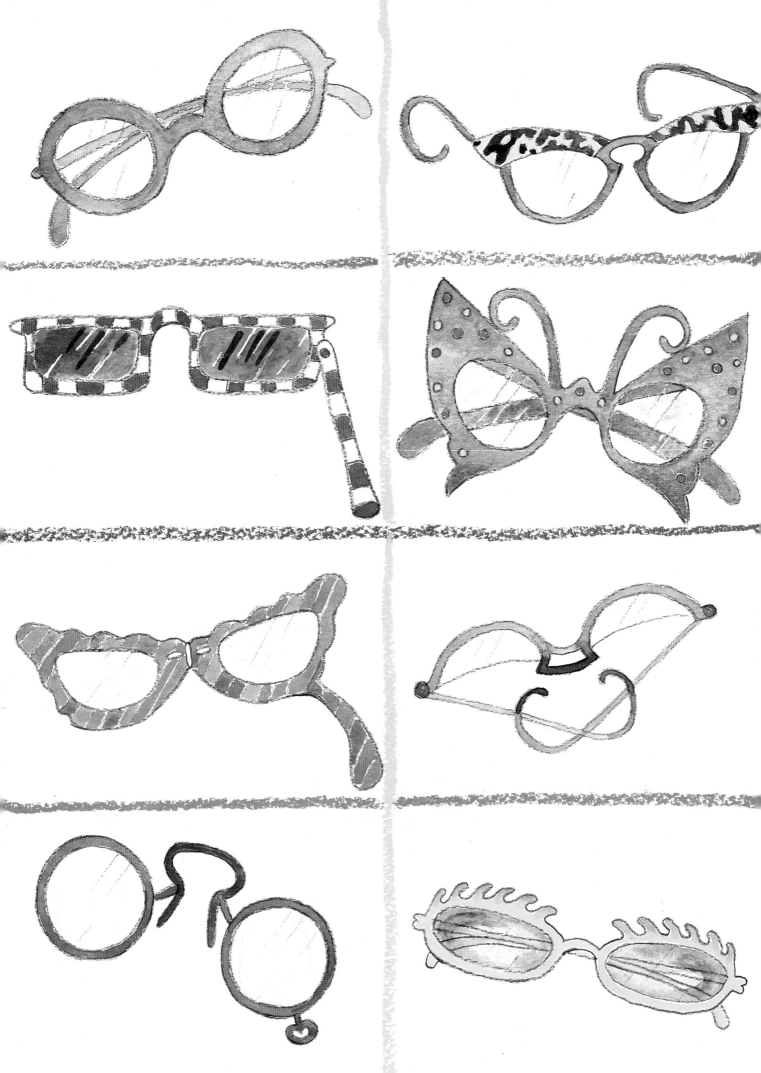

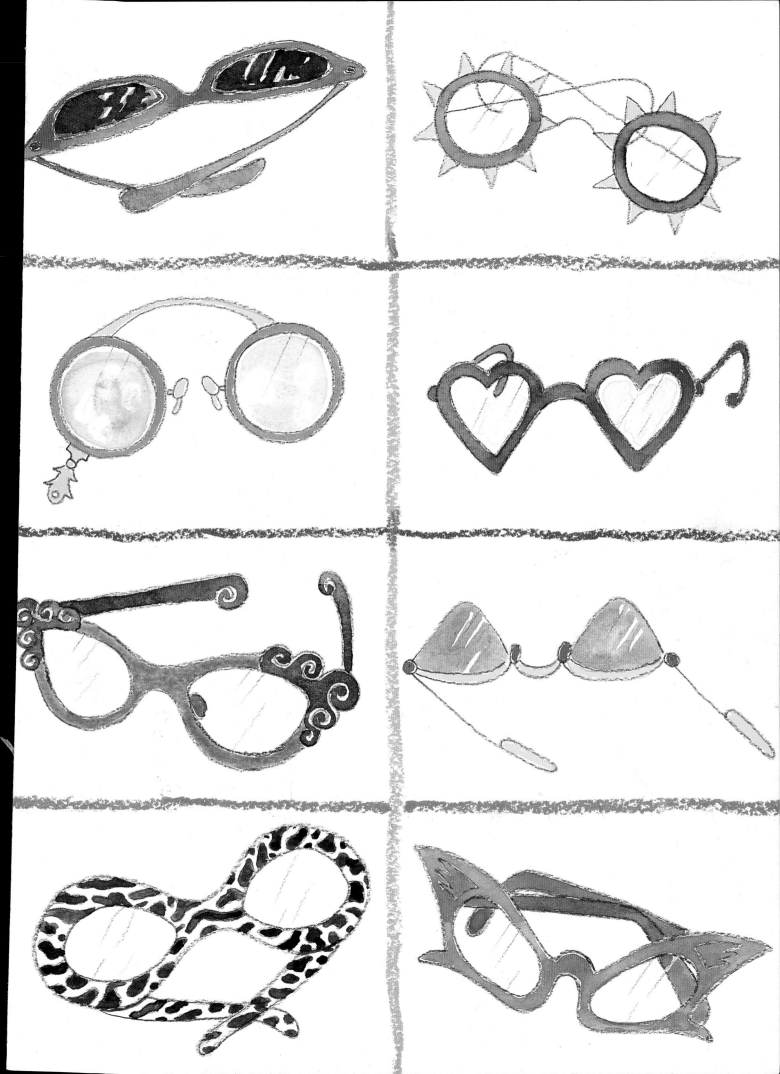